Ling Ling Bird
Hears
with his Magic Ears

Tanya Saunders

Ling Ling Bird has magic ears.

They help him to **hear.**

Listen!

He likes
listening to...

the busy **buzzy bees**,

buzz buzz buzz

the **wind blowing**
through the trees,

whoosh   whoosh

the brown **barking dog**

woof woof

and the green **hopping frog.**

hop hop hop

Ling Ling Bird likes
the big **moo cow**

moo moo moo

but not the **cat**
that says **meow.**

meow   meow

The **lion** is loud when it **roars**;

grrrr! grrrr!

so is the **crocodile**
snapping its jaws!

snap! snap! snap!

Even a tiny **mouse**
can **squeak**,

squeak squeak

and little **chicks** go
cheep cheep cheep.

cheep cheep cheep

Ling Ling Bird has a toy **train** -
choo choo, choo choo!

choo choo

and a pet **owl** -
hoo hoo, hoo hoo.

hoo hoo

This **man** likes to **laugh** - *haa haa haa!*

haa haa haa

Sheep don't laugh,
they just go **baa.**

baa baa baa

This **lady** has a red **car**

beep   beep

and a crying **baby** -
wah wah wah!

wah wah wah

shhh shhh

All day long
Ling Ling Bird
listens
to the
many sounds
that he **hears**
with his
super
magic ears.

buzz buzz

squeak squeak

baa baa

woof woof

moo moo

hop hop

cheep cheep

hoo hoo

beep beep

meow meow

grrr grrr

choo choo

Now he's **tired** -
it's time for **bed.**

yawn
yawn
yawn

"Come on **Ted!**"

teddy   teddy

Ling Ling Bird
likes the sound of
his Daddy's voice
when he says,
"I love you. Good night."

He likes
the sound of
his Mummy's kiss
when she says,
"I love you. Sleep tight."

Then he likes to **fall asleep**
under a silent moon
in the deep
dark
quiet
of his cosy bedroom.

About the Author

Having lived most of her life in the African wilderness with elephants literally on her doorstep, but now happily settled in the UK, Tanya Saunders is a writer, artist, lover of wild places and mother to twin daughters, one of whom is profoundly deaf and wears cochlear implants (her 'magic ears').

Tanya is a Parent Ambassador for Auditory Verbal UK (AVUK), an aspirational organisation that teaches deaf children to listen and speak. Her writing is inspired by her own family's speech and language journey with AVUK, alongside the numerous other specialists, friends and family members who, as a team, have made truly transformative contributions to her daughter's odyssey into the hearing and speaking world.

Although not a professional therapist herself, as a 'parent practitioner' of auditory verbal therapy traveling this road alongside her daughter, Tanya's personal experience and observations can provide helpful insights for other families on the same path. Her vibrantly illustrated stories encourage deaf children to reach for the stars and reassure them that, while it may not be easy, all the hard work involved in learning to listen and speak will be worth it in the end. Tanya blogs about parenting a deaf child at: **www.avidlanguage.com/hearsay-blog**

Ling Ling Bird Hears with his Magic Ears
Published by Avid Language Ltd, 3 Cam Drive, Ely, CB6 2WH, Cambridgeshire, UK
First published in 2020

ISBN
Paperback: 978-1-913968-03-8
Hardcover: 978-1-913968-04-5
eBook: 978-1-913968-05-2

Text and Illustrations copyright © Tanya Saunders 2020

Visit our website at: www.avidlanguage.com

AVID Language resources
Listen • Read • Speak • Practice • Play
www.avidlanguage.com

Follow the
Adventures of
Ling Ling Bird

 @LingLingBirdAdventures

 @LingBird

 @LingLingBirdAdventures

This one's for Emma and all at AVUK x

Printed in Great Britain
by Amazon